THE TUI
AN

RAFAELA CONTRERAS was born in San José, Costa Rica, on 21 May 1869 and died in San Salvador on 26 January 1893. She became the first wife of her childhood friend Rubén Darío, the Nicaraguan poet known for beginning the *modernismo* movement. After the death of her first son left her ill, Contreras returned to San Salvador to be close to her family, and in 1893 died there during an operation. Her known literary output consists of nine stories that were published in newspapers in El Salvador and Guatemala, but never in book form during her lifetime..

JESSICA SEQUEIRA is a writer and translator currently living in Santiago de Chile. Her works include the novel *A Furious Oyster* (Dostoyevsky Wannabe), the collection of stories *Rhombus and Oval* (What Books) and the collection of essays *Other Paradises: Poetic Approaches to Thinking in a Technological Age* (Zero Books). Her translations into English include Adolfo Couve's *When I Think of My Missing Head*, Hilda Mundy's *Pyrotechnics*, Liliana Colanzi's *Our Dead World*, Maurice Level's *The Gates of Hell*, Sara Gallardo's *Land of Smoke*, Teresa Wilms Montt's *In the Stillness of Marble*, and an anthology of stories by contemporary Chilean writers.

SNUGGLY BOOKS

RAFAELA CONTRERAS

THE TURQUOISE RING
AND OTHER STORIES

TRANSLATED AND WITH AN INTRODUCTION BY
JESSICA SEQUEIRA

THIS IS A SNUGGLY BOOK

ISBN: 978-1-64525-006-7

Contents

Introduction

THE nine stories by Rafaela Contreras, published in newspapers in El Salvador and Guatemala, but never in book form during her lifetime, take on a number of philosophical themes in an almost fairytale-like style. Her approaches suggest a proto-*modernismo* that in some ways anticipates the literary line that her husband, Rubén Darío, would explicitly develop, but also contain elements that might have taken a different direction, given more time. Contreras's work is concerned with the difference between the appearance of happiness and true happiness, the ability to see past illusion to truth, the desire for other places as opposed to the desire to stay at home, the sensitivity of impressions left in childhood, the changes in emotions and seasons, the importance of objects that give rise to reminiscence, and the influence of environment on a personality. Many of her stories include other stories within them, emphasizing the linked nature of human lives.

In many ways, Contreras's work is similar to that of her husband Rubén Darío, who was highly influenced by the symbolism of the French Parnassians. The question of whether Darío influenced Contreras, or vice versa, or whether 'influence' is an appropriate word for shared context, simultaneous growth and the mutual irrigation of love, passion and disillusionment in two people, is, however, tricker to parse. The emotional and aesthetic factors that go into writing can be mysterious, and hard facts (such as the order of publication dates) do not always reflect the origins of creative process. Matters are complicated by the fact that Darío, with his newspapers and connections, was responsible for finding Contreras the places where she could print her work, determining where and when the stories appeared.

That Darío's first stories date from 1885, five years before Contreras's first story, may suggest one truth; yet it is also true that until Darío met Contreras, his production was primarily focused on poetry, rather than prose. Just prior to the short period between 1890-91 when Contreras's work was being published in newspapers, Darío released his most famous work, *Azul...*, which includes ten 'Cuentos en prosa' [Stories in Prose]. Without diaries or documents to register their literary ideas, speculation is difficult; what is clear, however, is that whatever the similar background that informed the couple's themes or superficial overlaps in their literary approach, the two remained different writers. Contreras's stories are written in a key of her own, and the stylized cruelty and purified language on which she draws are shot through with greater tenderness. One wonders the direction she would have developed her writing, had she lived longer than her twenty-three years.

Rafaela Contreras Cañas was born in San José, Costa Rica, on 21 May 1869 and died in San Salvador on 26 January 1893. She was the daughter of Álvaro de Contreras, a Honduran public orator and man of political prestige, and Manuela Cañas, a Costa Rican of distinguished lineage, a descendant of the last Spanish governor Don José Manuel de Cañas. She became the first wife of her childhood friend Rubén Darío, the Nicaraguan poet known for beginning the *modernismo* movement. After the death of her first son left her weak and ill, Contreras returned to San Salvador to be close to her family, and in 1893 died there during an operation.

Contreras and Darío had known one another since their childhoods in León, when they met at the house of his aunt Rita de Rubén. Don Álvaro Contreras, Rafaela's father, had arrived in Nicaragua with his wife and two daughters after being exiled from Costa Rica for his role as a militant and defender of the Central American Union. Contreras and Darío would play together in the big old house that belonged to Darío's great-aunt Bernarda Sarmiento.

When Darío was seventeen years old he moved to El Salvador, sent by friends in Managua to avoid a possible marriage to his then-girlfriend Rosario Emelina Murillo. He remained in El Salvador from August 1882 until November 1883, when he returned to Nicaragua. During these months, Darío's friendship with Francisco Gavidia led him to study the French alexandrine in depth, and to develop his poetic style. He also often visited the Contreras household, and he attended the funeral of don Álvaro Contreras on 9 October 1882.

After another journey by Darío in June 1886 to Chile, again to avoid his first girlfriend, he published the novel *Emelina* in collaboration with Eduardo Poirier; its name refers to this same woman. He also published the poems *Abrojos* [Thistles], which contain existential and melancholy mediations similarly provoked by the failed relationship. Darío's most famous book of stories and poems *Azul . . .* , greatly influenced by his readings of French poetry, first appeared in Valparaíso in 1888.

The poet returned to Nicaragua on 6 March 1889, but quickly left again due to yet further difficulties with his Emelina, arriving in El Salvador on 1 May of that same year. The next month, in Santiago de Chile, his friend Pedro Balmaceda Toro died. Darío began to write the biography of this friend, to whom he referred by the pseudonym A. de Gilbert, and he finished writing it on 1 January 1890. While in Nicaragua, he helped to set up the newspaper *La Unión*, which first began to print on 7 November 1889. Darío himself served as editor, and financing came from the Nicaraguan president, General Francisco Menéndez.

The first story written by Rafaela Contreras, titled 'Mira la oriental o La mujer de cristal' (tr. in this edition as 'The Glass Woman'), appeared in Darío's newspaper *La Unión* in issue nº 178, on 10 February 1890. She signed it with the pseudonym Emelina. Some intense emotional overlap is suggested here, given that this was the name of Darío's first girlfriend. In any case, this pseudonym was used only once. A month later, on 10 March, a second story

10

by Contreras appeared in *La Unión*, titled 'Rêverie', which was signed with the pseudonym Stella, and accompanied by this evocative note written by Darío:

A HUMBLE FRAME

FOR

A CANVAS OF GOLD

In immense Paris—before leaving, and at the last five o'clock session of the beautiful Madame de Lucon—there, where I went to meet poor Jean de Lucon—her husband—one noticed something particular that afternoon. Orchids in vases and azaleas on the chest were in fashion. Near the sofa where Stella was accustomed to taking her seat—who did not know this—one saw a Sevres cup full of violets, and there, the adorable princess Stella had also pinned a spray of violets, very near to her heart.

You say that you would like to know about the princess Stella. Then I will say nothing to you except that we called her such because she was gentle, astral and sparkling like those white and trembling daisies that bloom in the night, in the divine blue garden. Oh, she had a great deal of the dominant, amidst a sly ingenuousness that at times transformed into the silvery cascade of vibrant chatter. In the house of Madame de Lucon, she was the beautiful Madame de Montbleu with her tender blue eyes, which swam in a gently radiant humidity: not even the pretty mademoiselle Carire, so frivolous and elegant, drew the attention of all so much as that strange look, that dark and flashing gaze with such depth, and that triumphant expression. For this reason we called her: S t e l l a.

With those violets! Everybody dreamed up a novel for her in his head. During the entire gathering, the matter was spoken of sotto voce. What did those violets mean?

We thought, we thought a great deal. No one gave up, and upon withdrawing after the joy of time pleasantly spent, phrases were made 'with the violets of Stella'.

Only Jean Lucon had not opened his lips. With my curiosity about women, I approached him.

Well, Jean, what about the violets?

Then he spoke to me of Stella. She was a strange, original and radiant soul. Don't you know? for after our poor glorious deceased Jeanne Thilda, there is no one like her for writing about things from 'here'. And Jean touched his heart. She is, as you know, the daughter of an illustrious man of letters. The law of heredity. As for your curiosity about the bouquet of violets, I will tell you nothing, because I know little: it is her flower. Do you want to know more? Then ask her.

※

Then ask her! and I went and was able to become her confidant, satisfying my curiosities. Do you want to satisfy yours, oh reader? Then I have here a story that I have selected from those which will soon appear in a volume by Stella, published by the editor Garnier.

Its title is *RÊVERIE*.

I know that after the publication of that first book which contains this story, Stella will give the public a delicate and artistic novel, full of femininity. Look at the story which immediately follows.

RUBÉN DARÍO

'Rêverie' was the title of Rafaela Contreras's second piece, the same title that Darío used to announce the upcoming publication of a collection of her stories.

The title and pseudonym 'Stella' were both inventions of Darío. Although Darío claimed that the book would be published by the well-known editor Garnier in Paris, however, the book never came out. Whether this was due to Contreras's early death or to her not having yet finished the book, and if the latter is the case, whether this was because she hoped to add more stories or because she had lost interest in writing after her marriage, is to this day ambiguous. Commentators have offered different explanations based on dubious or non-existent evidence, but the mystery lingers.

In June 1890, the newspaper *La Unión* ceased to publish, due to an order by the government. On 21 June, Contreras and Darío were joined in civil matrimony at the bride's house, with the poet Francisco Gavidia and *La Unión*'s former editor-in-chief Tranquilino Chacón as witnesses. That same night, a military coup took place, headed by General Ezeta, who took power after assassinating President Menéndez. On 27 June, Darío left alone from the port La Libertad for Guatemala, where he arrived three days later. Almost immediately he began to collaborate with the *Diario de Centro América*. On 30 October 1890 a second expanded edition of *Azul . . .* was released.

During this time, Darío continued to promote Contreras's work. When *El Imparcial* in Guatemala introduced one of Contreras's stories in its 22 and 23 July 1890 editions, it referred to her as an 'escritora de raza' [born writer]. In the 11 and 18 October editions of *El Perú Ilustrado*, at that time one of the most widely-read publications in Latin America, with José

Santos Chocano, Manuel Gutiérez Nájera and Ricardo Palma among its contributors, the story 'Violetas y palomas' was accompanied by a note:

> Rubén Darío has visited Peru and Chile in the not-distant past and been united in matrimony with a very distinguished writer, who under the pseudonym of 'Stella' has until now carried solace and joy to the homes of our writers. Today she will continue to do so in her own name: Rafaela de Darío, bringing beauty to our weekly with productions like 'Violetas y palomas', which we are printing in serialized form.

In the meantime, Darío began to organize the newspaper *El Correo de la Tarde* in Guatemala, the first issue of which came out on 8 December 1890. On 12 January 1891 Darío was reunited with Contreras, when she arrived in that country with her mother. On 11 February they celebrated their religious wedding at a cathedral in Guatemala, and celebrated again with friends the next day in the city of Escuintla. Unfortunately, the newspaper that Darío was working on faced obstacles that it could not overcome. On 5 June, number 141 of *El Correo de la Tarde* appeared, the final issue. Due to their economic difficulties, the family left for the port of San José, stopping in Puntarenas with a final destination of Costa Rica. In San José, on 12 November 1891, their son Rubén Darío Contreras was born, the only son of Darío's who would survive.

After a few months, on 11 May 1892, Darío left for Guatemala. It was the last time that he saw his wife, who left soon after for San Salvador with her mother and their son. Darío continued to travel, returning to Nicaragua, passing through La Habana and arriving in Spain, as secretary of the delegation of his country to the celebrations of the fourth centenary of America's discovery. He remained there for several months, from August to November. After stopping again in La Habana, he visited Colombia and arrived in Nicaragua on 5 January 1893. A few days later, on 26 January, Rafaela Contreras died in San Salvador during an operation, a result of cerebral hemorrhage.

The following poem by Rubén Darío, a tribute to his recently deceased wife, appeared in the Buenos Aires newspaper *La Tribuna* on 9 October 1893, under the title 'Lilial'. Later it was published in his book *Prosas profanas* in 1896, under the title 'El poeta pregunta por Stella'. Here is the poem in my translation:

The Poet Asks about Stella

Divine lily, lily of the Annunciations;
                              lily, flowery prince,
perfumed brother to the chaste stars,
                              jewel of Aprils.

For you the white Dianas in ducal parks;
the necks of swans,
the mystic verses of celestial hymns
and the hands of virgins in the sacred Empyrean.

16

Lily, snowy mouth on which springtime
presses her sweet lips:
in your veins there runs not the blood
                              of sinful roses,
but the lofty ichor of illustrious flowers.

Royal and lyrical lily,
you who are born with the whiteness
                              of sublime hosts,
of gleaming pearls
and the immaculate linen of surplices:
Have you by any chance seen in flight the soul
                              of my Stella,
sister to Ligeia, on whose account my song
                              is sometimes so sad?

During her own lifetime, Contreras was almost always thought of by other writers as the wife of Darío, not as a writer herself. One exception is the Peruvian novelist Clorinda Matto de Turner, who said of Contreras in a discussion of Central American women authors in *Búcaro Americano* (Buenos Aires, 1 February 1896) that 'the sympathetic and cherished name of Rafaela de Darío elegantly responds to the contemporary history of Guatemala'.

Rafaela's writing, as mentioned, does show traces of interests similar to those of Darío. Her first eight stories were written in 1890, with seven seeing the light a little more than a year after the publication of *Azul . . . ,*

17

which first appeared in July 1888. The Nicaraguan literary critic Ricardo Llopesa even makes the argument that Contreras was 'the first recipient of the influence of the first modernist book, which in turn makes her the first modernist writer'. He notes that 'The Glass Woman', with its 'oriental atmosphere, exoticism and idol worship by man for an image' complements Darío's story 'The Death of the Empress of China'. Although Rafaela's story came out earlier, on 10 February 1890 as opposed to Darío's 15 May, a difference of two months and five days, he writes that there is a document by Gustavo Alemán Bolaños referring to a story read by Darío at Rubén Rivera's house, in August of the previous year. In other words, he argues that Darío's work preceded Contreras's work. Whether or not this is true, Contreras's work is not Darío's work, and possesses emotional subtleties that rewrite the symbolist and imagistic themes she works into her own register.

Due to the fact that the newspapers where Contreras published her work were small and poorly circulated, with several folding within her lifetime, and given that she never left behind a book that gathered together her stories, her work fell into oblivion after her death. Two of the stories, 'La canción del invierno' and 'Sonata', were even included by Alberto Ghiraldo and Andrés González Blanco in their 1924 Afrodisio Aguado edition of Rubén Darío's *Obras completas* published in Madrid, a false attribution of her work to her husband.

Contreras's stories have had a slow-burning afterlife. Two main investigators are responsible for rediscovering them. The first is the Nicaraguan lawyer Dr Diego Manuel Sequeira, who studied in Paris and was also interested in literature. Looking into the two stays of Rubén Darío in El Salvador, and trying to find out more about the woman behind Darío's poem *El poeta pregunta por Stella*, he discovered the stories of Contreras, and was able to compile six of the pieces she wrote under the pseudonym *Stella*, published in the San Salvador newspaper *La Unión* between February and May 1890. His research culminated in the 1964 book *Rubén Darío criollo en El Salvador*, which printed the six stories and briefly discussed the works.

The other important researcher was Dr Evelyn Uhrhan Irving. In 1960, as a professor at Macalester College in Saint Paul, Minnesota, she moved to Guatemala to take a better look at Contreras's work. There, in newspaper archives, she discovered three stories that had not appeared in Sequeira's book. In 1965 she published *Short Stories by Rafaela Contreras de Darío*, gathering seven stories in Spanish (the preface is from June 1964). 'La turquesa' and 'Humanzor', which appear in Sequeira, are missing, but 'Violetas y palomas', 'Sonata' and 'El oro y el cobre' are presented in book form for the first time.

All nine stories by Contreras had thus been discovered, if the Sequeira and Uhrhan Irving editions are taken together. This strange disparity was rectified in a second edition by Uhrhan Irving, published several decades later in 1995 by the Fundación Rubén Darío in Nicaragua, under the title *Nueve cuentos de Rafaela Contreras*. The work of Sequeira and Uhrhan Irving was given attention in a newspaper article by Emilia del Romero in the Mexican newspaper *El Nacional* on 19 June 1966, discussing the discovery of the nine stories and their context. From this moment Contreras's work began to be noted more frequently in academic and journalistic literature, although unlike Darío, Contreras is still unknown to the general public.

The present edition is the first English translation of the stories of Rafaela Contreras. They not only serve as a valuable document offering a personal version of the literary movements of the period, but also offer a series of flights of the imagination that are fanciful, entertaining and moving by turns, embarking on unusual and subtle forays into different realms of human experience, in the author's own tones. As Uhrhan Irving put it, 'We find in these stories characteristics of Modernism, the exotic and supernatural. Whereas Darío wrote that he concentrated the spiritual flowering of his artistic spring in the color *azul*, it is evident that Rafaela symbolized hers with *violeta*.'

—Jessica Sequeira

Note on the Text

The stories have been arranged in this volume in a way that we feel presents them best, rather than in strict chronological order; their original dates of publication are listed below:

—'Mira la oriental o la mujer de cristal'. *La Unión*, San Salvador, 10 February 1890; *El Imparcial*, Guatemala, 31 July and 2 August 1890, signed *Emelina*.
—'Rêverie'. *La Unión*, San Salvador, 10 March 1890; *El Perú Ilustrado*, Lima, 17 May 1890, signed *Stella*; *El Imparcial*, Guatemala, 24 July 1890, signed *Rafaela de Darío*.
—'La turquesa'. *La Unión*, San Salvador, 22 April 1890; *El Imparcial*, Guatemala, 9 and 10 November 1890, signed *Stella*.
—'Las ondinas'. *Repertorio Salvadoreño*, vol. IV, nº 4, April 1890, pp. 207-216, signed *Stella*.
—'Humanzor'. *La Unión*, San Salvador, 5 May 1890, signed *Stella*.
—'La canción del invierno'. *La Unión*, San Salvador, 19 May 1890, signed *Stella*.

—'Violetas y palomas'. *El Imparcial*, Guatemala, 22 and 23 July 1890. Signed *Rafaela de Darío*; *El Perú Ilustrado*, Lima, 11 and 18 October 1890, signed *Rafael de Darío*.

—'Sonata'. *El Correo de la Tarde*, Guatemala, 27 December 1890, signed *Stella*.

—'El oro y el cobre'. El Correo de la Tarde, Guatemala, 8 April 1891, signed *Stella*.

Sources:

—Darío, Rubén ed. Stanley Appelbaum. *Cuentos y poesías*. Dover Publications, 2002.

—Llopesa, Ricardo. 'Rafaela Contreras, primera escritora modernista'. 18 July 2018. *Letralia*.

—Sánchez, María Teresa. *El poeta pregunta por Stella*. Managua. Editorial Nuevos Horizontes, 1967.

—Sequeira, Diego Manuel, *Rubén Darío criollo en El Salvador*. León (Nicaragua), Editorial Hospicio, 1964, pp. 353-435.

—Uhrhan Irving, Evelyn. Introduction to *Short Stories by Rafaela Contreras de Darío*. Miami. University of Miami Press, 1965; *Nueve cuentos de Rafaela Contreras* (second edition). Managua. Fundación Rubén Darío, 1995.

THE TURQUOISE RING
AND OTHER STORIES

The Turquoise Ring

ANGELO was free at last. He was twenty-one years old, had the greatest amount of capital in Naples and held the title of Marquis de Castelfiore. He was a truly seductive young man, handsome like the majority of those born under the blue sky of beautiful Italy. His heart was a pearl of incalculable value, and he was gifted with great virtues; unfortunately, however, his head was rather light. Thus once he had finished his period of mourning for the deceased Marquis, his father, he threw himself into that whirlwind from which so rarely one emerges unscathed, called 'society'. His beauty and his figure were two entrance cards of a value rarely found in any other form. The world opened its monstrous mouth, and the inexperienced young man plunged into it, eager for pleasure.

Angelo amused himself, and how! He was always content, always smiling and happy. And his mother, the good and virtuous Marchioness, smiled at seeing him and took pleasure in his satisfaction. Angelo was spoiled. Men enjoyed his money; for women he was a magnificent catch.

In his palaces, gold, silver and bronze in silver-ware and statues could be seen. Lamps of rich porcelain or alabaster, gardens of marble and columns of porphyry gleamed everywhere. Feasts were given in which champagne flowed in as much plenty as the gold on the gaming tables. In the forests on his property there were frequent hunts, attended by the nobility. Angelo was the most powerful lord in Naples. Regrettably, he came to understand this, and an intoxication more powerful than alcohol overwhelmed his brain.

'Angelo,' a friend said to him one day, 'have you noticed something?'

'What?'

'Lucrecia is in love with you.'

'Bah!' he said, letting out a loud laugh, 'it seems that even the ugly ones dare to love me.'

'And you?'

'Me? I let myself be loved! I love only the little duchess of Rossi.'

'Well then! And is she your betrothed?'

'I should think.'

'Poor Lucrecia!'

Lucrecia was a young woman of nineteen years old, delicate, extremely thin and pale; her eyes were very beautiful, black and shining; her hair was chestnut-colored, short and very straight; she had a straight and classical nose, and an adorable mouth. Her heart was that of an angel, and she was gifted with particular sensibility. She was quite poor but belonged to the nobility.

She lived with her maternal grandmother, for her parents had died. The Marchioness, Angelo's mother, loved the poor girl very much, and it was there, in his own house, that she met the young man. She understood the qualities that adorned him, she saw his real beauty and loved him with all the strength of a heart as large as hers was, and all the stoicism of the Abnegation, for believing herself to be extremely small, she loved him without the aspiration of being rewarded. However, she could not keep her secret in such a way that no one discovered it. The living fire of her gaze when she was near the young man revealed it. So it was that the friend of the Marquis, who was very suspicious, came to understand this young woman's passion, and later mocked her.

Time spent in such a mad way felt to Angelo like brief moments. Thus he did not see how in such a short time he could have used up half his fortune, and when his mother warned him, he shrugged his shoulders dismissively and answered:

'I'll recover it. Don't pay it any attention.'

One day, strolling alone about the outskirts of Naples, he saw several girls from town and some young men surrounding a mob of gypsies, who sold pendants, necklaces, earrings and a thousand other trinkets, to which they attributed particular qualities that could influence the destiny of those who always wore them. He came near and began to listen to the gypsy seller.

'The one who always wears this necklace will keep his youth while he lives. A florin and it stays with one of you.'

The necklace sold or rejected, he heard the shout again:

'Here is a brooch that has the virtue of winning the love of whoever is desired by the one who comes to be its owner.'

The brooch was sold immediately, for all the girls fought over it.

'This ring is a magnificent turquoise. It will preserve the one who constantly wears it from being deceived by anyone, for it gives double sight. He who possesses it will see into the depths of consciences and the most profound recesses of the heart of all those around him.'

This seemed curious to Angelo and he threw a pocketful of escudos to the gypsy. Then he moved away, putting the turquoise on his hand.

At night he had promised to see his social circle. When eight struck he headed out, without taking off the turquoise ring, which he did not even remember.

When he entered, upon seeing him, a group of his acquaintances came out to greet him. One of them said:

'My dear Angelo! We were waiting for you and were already starting to grow worried, fearing that you were not coming. You know how much we care about you.'

The Marquis stopped when the young man started to speak, and looked at him fixedly, listening with signs of marked terror and fury.

'But what has happened to you?' the young man spoke again, stretching out his hand. Angelo rejected it, shouting: 'Leave me.' And turning his back brusquely on all those who, full of astonishment, watched him move away, he headed toward the hall to meet others.

He arrived, greeted them and sat down, frightened by what he had read in the conscience of that one who had first addressed him. What was it? 'How does it matter to me if you come or not, if I detest you because you are more handsome and have more gold than we do? But I must flatter you, for at your cost we amuse ourselves so!'

This he saw as if it were written behind that smile of friendly affection and that seemingly honest face.

'Angelo, I see you looking sad. You have sorrows, you, whom all love for your goodness and superb clothing,' another said.

He looked at him and read:

'You have sorrows, you, who always hear flattering comments, because you are rich and stupid enough to squander your gold on banquets to treat us!'

He stood up and, without giving any answer, headed out half-crazed toward the street. Once there, he started to walk at random, without knowing what to do. After a long time, he stopped at a corner, from which he then moved away, desperate, for he saw many people pass, who, upon noticing him, said smiling:

'Good evening, Sr. Marquis, I am very happy to see you.'

'Hello, Angelo! How is your health? It's been days since I've seen you and I feared you were ill. Goodbye, Marquis, may you amuse yourself greatly.'

And like these came many other declarations of affection and friendship, after which he read:

'I would never like to see you again because I loathe you.'—'I believed you were sick and was happy, because I am envious of you. You are beautiful and rich, while I am ugly and poor.'

Two tears of fire burned his cheeks, but he thought of his betrothed and said to himself: 'I'll go to her!'

This idea calmed him somewhat and he took the road to the house of his beloved. He entered, still a bit sad, but upon seeing her so beautiful, he forgot everything and smiled again, now content. 'My dear Adela,' he said to her, 'I want to move our union forward. It is impossible for me to wait any longer. Do you wish for this too?'

'Yes, Angelo; you already know with what yearning I await that moment. I love you so much.'

He looked at her, and, terrified, he read: 'I wish to marry you because you are the most handsome man in Naples, and, above all, the richest. The others are jealous of me and this flatters my vanity, which is the most important thing. I love you because I love myself.'

He rose, pale as a dead man and, stretching out his hand to the young woman, said to her:

'I feel overcome by a sudden indisposition. Goodbye.'

'Really? You upset me, Angelo. Take great care of yourself: I don't want you to get sick.'

He nailed his eyes on her, scrutinized the most hidden places of her heart, and full of bitterness, saw that those phrases had merely sprung up on her lips. In her interior was complete indifference.

The unhappy young man went out staggering, as if he were drunk. He arrived at his house, entered his bedroom without seeing anyone, shut himself away with a key, and let himself fall into an armchair. There, with his head between his hands, he remained for a long time, completely forgetting the world. Everything had disappeared for him: he did not see, nor did he think, except lethargically. It was midnight when he came to his senses. Then he removed the turquoise from his hand, the cause of his tragedy, and after putting it on the nightstand, went back to sit down, starting to cry in a desperate way. After he had vented his sorrows a little, he began to reflect with greater calm. Hope, that companion which should never abandon man, took up its place in the heart of the young man.

Not wanting to fool himself, however, he was determined to touch reality before anything else, and so he sketched out a plan for himself, his heart filled with bile; he promised himself to have courage, and he lay down as day was already breaking, exhausted from so many terrible emotions.

The next day no one would have suspected that the poor young man had suffered, not only suffered but meditated. For a month he seemed so splendidly obliging and spendthrift that he produced admiration in all, and terror in his mother. At the end of this period, he shut himself away one night in his bedroom, got into bed and ordered the doctor to be called. His mother asked to come see him, but he did not wish to allow her visit in any way. He remained speaking with the doctor for a long time, who afterward went straight to see the marchioness, whom he found crying. When he left, the good lady was happy and entirely calm. The next day, everyone knew that Angelo had been seized by smallpox, and added that he would be horribly disfigured. Everyone went to find out about him, however, and his betrothed did not miss a single day in her visits to the Marchioness, to personally obtain news of his health. For many days he was in bed, and when at last he rose, his face was completely covered with a kind of mask that he said the doctor had ordered him to put on.

One night he sent to have his carriage made ready and went to see his beloved, always wearing the mask and also the turquoise ring. When he entered, he saw the horrified movement of all those gathered, but he pretended that he had not noticed it, as sitting alongside Adela, he said to her in a low voice: 'Dear Adela, I have come to see you like this, because I could no longer resist after so long.'

'Ah,' she answered, 'and me?'

He smiled at her without answering; he had read:

'What horror! Better if you hadn't come!'

'I am very sad,' he continued, 'because I fear that you no longer love me. I have been horribly disfigured. If you could only see me!'

She went pale, but recovered and answered: 'And what does it matter to me if you are or aren't disfigured? Do I love you for your face alone?'

He smiled again, for he saw in reality that it was not so much for his face that she accepted him, as for his wealth. He was the richest man in the city, and she saw him covered by a mask of gold. He trembled with spite.

※

A month passed, and still he did not remove the mask. During this time, news spread that the Marquis was ruined, and that his palaces, the last remainder of his fortune, were going to pass into the hands of a stranger. Everyone ran to see him and learn what had happened at the house of the Marquis, and he confessed that the rumors were true. Just afterward, the owners of the palace went to inhabit a rented house, modestly arranged. There Angelo received a letter from Adela in which she formally broke their engagements, for according to what she said, a man who had wasted his capital in such a way would not be in her best interest.

He had put on his turquoise, and therefore could see clearly. He stood up when he finished reading the letter and went to see his mother, whom he found with Lucrecia, the poor orphan with an ugly face but the soul of an angel.

'Mother, read this,' he said, handing over the letter.

The good lady read, and two tears rolled down her cheeks. She opened her arms and hugged her son between them.

He looked at her, moved, and asked her:

'And you aren't going to say anything else? Aren't you going to direct recriminations at me like they are all doing today?'

'No, my son,' she answered, 'you must already be suffering so much, and if by being poor you return to the good path and understand what the world is, I will consider myself blessed in my poverty. My affection will never be lacking, for the love of a mother increases instead of decreases when misfortune afflicts her son.'

The words of the Marchioness were sincere, like those of every good mother; this he understood, and his eyes shone with tears.

'What's more,' she continued, 'a friend remains to us, good Lucrecia, who loves us sincerely and disinterestedly.'

The poor girl, red with shame, lowered her eyes upon hearing this praise, but when she lifted them, Angelo looked at her deeply and asked:

'Is that true, Lucrecia? You don't hold me in contempt, you don't flee from me?'

'No, my friend,' she answered; 'what has happened to you is purely misfortune; but you are young and have good sentiments, and you can, with courage and determination, recover what has been lost.'

'And my face that is now hideous, how to fix that?'

'Why should it matter to you if it's beautiful or not? Is it only for beauty that one can appreciate and love you?'

'You are right,' he said, moved by the loyalty, virtue and grandeur of a girl whom God had not given much beauty, but had given an angelical goodness and superior intelligence.

For many days Angelo remained without leaving his poor dwelling, and when he did so at last, he went by foot for a walk through the city. Some of his old friends noticed him; there were even some who walked right past him, but no one acknowledged or greeted him. Now he was no longer rich; he was almost a beggar.

He returned home, where he found Lucrecia with his mother, which made him feel true pleasure and great consolation. He said as much to her, and the poor girl, almost crying with pleasure, thanked him. This great, generous being loved him in spite of everything! The knowledge of such disinterested passion made a profound love spring up in the heart of Angelo for the poor orphan, whose only wealth was the strength of her soul. He confessed this, and listened to the promise come from her lips that she would join herself to him, whom she loved so much. He then made sure that everyone knew it, and informed himself of what was said. Everyone laughed, saying that only Lucrecia was capable of uniting in marriage with a man with a hideous face and empty pockets.

Preparing everything, and without saying anything to either his mother or his beloved, he had invitations distributed to all the nobility, who received them with great astonishment, for the address on the card was that of the old palace, the almost royal dwelling that Angelo had previously inhabited. On the eve of his wedding, he sent for a carriage and brought his mother and Lucrecia, who were amazed, to his old dwelling, as he told them the story of the turquoise ring and confessed to them that everything that had happened was a farce, to convince himself of whom his friends were in prosperity and adversity.

He then pulled off the mask and his handsome face appeared, as handsome as it had been before, for the illness had not been real either.

On the second day, all came with haste to the palace, full of curiosity. Mute with admiration, they saw Angelo appear as handsome as ever and dressed as usual with Asiatic luxury, bearing on his arm Lucrecia, whom happiness had transformed and made appear almost beautiful in the midst of the riches in which she was decked.

No one stayed without going to give congratulations to Angelo, who smiled with such irony that he made all the faces blush or go pale.

When the immense procession entered the church, by chance it passed Adela de Rossi, the former betrothed of the Marquis. He saw her and, casting her a glance of contempt and a mocking smile, greeted her. All turned their faces and also smiled, as they thought about what the woman must be suffering. Half mad with spite, envy and rage, she went through the first door she found, and waited there hidden until the retinue disappeared into the temple.

That same day, in the afternoon, when everyone had already left, Angelo gave the turquoise to Lucrecia, asking her to put it on her hand when she wished to convince herself of his love. About the world, never; it was better to live in illusion.

From that day on, the parties and madnesses came to an end. Alone, loving one another forever and deeply, these two generous souls lived in the midst of the despicable, mean-spirited world, which in their happiness they forgot.

Violets and Doves

TOGETHER Ermelia and I, following the banks of the river, walked along gathering flowers, as the last houses disappeared from our sight.

And how many beautiful flowers there were! The forget-me-nots, the wallflowers, the bluebells! And the Danube, with its current similar to a great rippling serpent, kissed them with love. White foam like a duck feather caressed their petals.

My exhausted friend, red like a poppy and with her brow damp with sweat, laughed madly and ran unceasingly after a new flower for her bouquet.

All of a sudden she stopped and breathed in with force, as if to assure herself there was some flower she still had not seen, but whose perfume she felt. Right afterward I saw her kneel on the damp grass and search with feverish impatience for something.

'What are you looking for?' I asked, when I saw that she was not finding the object of her longing.

She did not answer me but continued her investigation, dragging her dress of rose-colored percaline through the fresh green pasture.

I then saw her straighten up her bust of a princess, and join her hands as if she were going to pray, as two tears pure as dew in the calyx of a flower rolled down her burning cheeks.

Running to her, I questioned her again, but she pushed me aside with gentleness and said to me, smiling:

'Wait!'

She held aside the grass and began to cut a great many flowers. But do you know which? Violets! They were violets, those flowers at the sight of which Ermelia had shed her tears.

Undoubtedly there must exist a mystery I needed to clarify, not out of curiosity, but out of interest, as much in my friend as in that flower, my favorite flower.

When she finished, she stood up and, with a seriousness that was strange in her happy character, took me by the hand, saying:

'Come, Stella, and you will know a whole story, the story of a heart.'

'And the violets,' I asked her, 'won't you tell me anything about them?'

'It is precisely the story of a violet that you are going to hear.'

'But where?' I repeated. 'Don't you see that we have moved away quite a bit?'

'We are going to leave the river, and there where you see those trees, under the chestnut with wide branches, we will sit while I tell you the story.'

So it went. We left the Danube and the ferns of its banks and advanced into the bushes and trees, until we reached the foot of the chestnut, on whose ancient trunk we sat down, tired.

❋

It was more or less five in the afternoon when we arrived there. The sun hoisted up its dying light with its last vague gleams on the crowns of chestnuts and holm oaks, amidst whose majestic foliage the wind whistled to form a rhythmical harmony. There, in the neighboring forest, the nightingale let its melodious song be heard, which mingled with the thundering sound of the Danube that swept along its enormous mass of water.

Ermelia put her bouquet on a branch of the chestnut tree, and taking my hands between her white ones, held them tightly, effusively. Then she said:

'Listen, Stella, do you know what the violets are to me? The soul of a dead girl whom I loved very much, now even more than when she was still living.

'Her name was Arminda and I met her in Vienna, at the school where we were educated together.

'Later, one day, they took her from the school and brought her there,' she said, pointing to the road to Gross-Aspern.

'Her father, the poor old man whom she loved so much, her only support, had died when she was only thirteen years old!

'She was the daughter of one of those pale flowers that breathe out their tender and melancholy perfume in the spring afternoons, when the last rays of the sun gild them.

'There remained to her no one in the world but her elderly nursemaid, who, though full of ailments, cared for her and loved her as a daughter.

'She came, then, to live with her in the little house hidden amidst the leaves, kissed by the breeze and caressed by the doves that always sang on the slate roof, or made their nests in the branches of the orange trees, tucked away in the white and perfumed blossoms.

'Getting up very early, dressed in blue or pink, she went out to the garden for a stroll, while the breeze caressed her golden locks.

'The butterflies that flew over the flowers passed so close to her that they brushed the face of the madonna lily with their wings of gold and burgundy.

'Her greatest joy was to cut flowers, many flowers, which she fastened on her chest and in her blonde tresses.

'In the afternoon, when the sun was already beginning to hide its disc of fire there far away, on the horizon, she took the road along the river with Herman, a charming boy, blond like her, like her a dreamer and like her also an orphan, but only made so by his father.

'And the pretty and innocent couple went for long walks, always gathering the blue violets that grew there on the banks of the Danube, listening to the final song of the birds and seeing the dying reflection of day in the clouds that tinted the outlines of the horizon.

'When winter came with its cold winds, its gray sky and its fogs, when the birds were silent, the flowers withered, the trees lost their leaves and the ground was covered by a sheet of snow, Arminda read alongside the fire or knitted. Sometimes Herman came wrapped in a great cape to share the heat of the stove with his dear little friend, who looking through the windows of the room at the sad garb of nature, tried to copy it with her little paintbrush and its gloomy colors.'

⁂

'In this way time passed quickly. She turned sixteen; he twenty. The girl turned into a woman, the boy became a man. And always together, always seeing one another, the affection of first childhood was replaced by love.

'Then they understood the language of nature; what the white irises say to the daisies, the pansies to the violets and the spikenard to the mimosa; they understood what the turtledoves say as a loving couple; what the birds sing in the forest; what the breeze says to the brook of white foam when it plays at licking the fresh grass, what is said by the immense blue sky.

'He saw in the eyes of Arminda, in her curly locks, in her rosebud mouth, in her waist of a nymph, the image of happiness, the fount of his dreams, his aspirations, his hopes.

'She, on that clear brow, across which there seemed to cross lightning flashes of inspiration, in that brilliant gaze, saw the clarity of a celestial body and the tenderness of a great heart, her faith and her future.

'One day, as a slow and light rain fell, with the sky covered by lead-colored clouds and the trees without leaves, the wind hummed in a melancholy way alongside the windows of the little house, as she, near the unlit stove, remaining mute and unmoving, looking at Herman, who in his turn looked at her with pain. She cried without cease.

'He went away. He had to go in search of fortune, make a living, feed his elderly mother and then bring something to build that home of which they had dreamed, where Arminda, adored as 'God on the altar', would make him happy with her happiness.

'He left then, after making her a thousand promises of love and offering her a quick return.

'And while he crossed the blue waves, she wept with grief.

'Her weeping increased later, before the winter mists had disappeared: the elderly nursemaid died and the poor girl was left alone, completely alone, in the little house that the leaves hid, the sun gilded and the turtledoves caressed in spring. And winter was still the season that reigned outside the house and inside, and even more so, in the heart of the young woman.

'Arminda had lost weight in an extraordinary way: her blue eyes, previously sparkling and radiant, were sunken and shone only through the impulses of fever; she was pale and her golden locks made her seem a statue of marble with a helmet of gold. A constant fatigue tormented her.

'The birds sang and the doves cooed; the bees sipped the honey of the flowers and the sun bathed the little house with its warm rays. But the girl, indifferent and pensive, remained alone by the window, sewing.

'And dawn, which with its rosy fingers lifted the black chiffon of night, giving way to the light that fell on the earth, found her there, by the window, in the melancholy light of a lamp, sewing, always sewing.

'What was she sewing? A piece of embroidery on which she put flowers, and leaves withered like her, and birds that were mute, as those of the forest now seemed to her.

'Sewing always, at all hours, and at all hours crying, the unhappy one earned the piece of bread that her slim and transparent hands carried to her pale lips. And little by little that flower died, in the midst of the life and joy of nature. The cold north wind had lashed her harshly that winter!

'And in the meantime he worked without rest and wrote to her constantly, announcing his return.'

'Herman returned content; at last he had the means to carry out his dreams.

'He now saw the little house hidden amidst the leaves, he saw the doves warming themselves in the sun and the white daisies swayed by the breeze.

'Entering at a run, he looked for his lover but found only me, who had arrived the day before, crying alongside the white corpse, surrounded by violets and orange blossoms, and illuminated by four large candles that spluttered constantly.

'The poor flower had at last been cut!

'I handed Herman a great bunch of those violets that had a blue color, and said to him:

'"She has given me this bunch for you, entrusting me to tell you that you will find her spirit in the perfume of this flower as weak as she was."

'A howl replied to my last words. Herman pulled the violets from my hand, kissed them and, holding them tightly against his heart, exclaimed:

'"Yes, it's true. The perfume of the violets is her soul that kisses and caresses me!"

'The next day he and I followed the path along the river, walking after the modest coffin that enclosed the remains of the pale girl.

'Afterward we parted ways, and I never saw him again.'

'I, fulfilling the final wishes of my dead friend, planted alongside her tomb, around the modest cross, many violets that now grow and bloom, lushly radiant.

'Do you want to see where she sleeps the eternal dream?'

'Yes,' I answered.

'Let's go,' she said, standing. And clasping each other's hands we embarked on the road to the city.

We did not go very far. On a very small hill alongside the road, the modest cross signaled to us the tomb.

I went down on my knees, cut some violets and breathed their pleasing fragrance.

She was right! Something like an infinite love, but sad, the love of a being more noble than usual, this was the essence that penetrated and moved even the last fiber of the heart.

Ermelia was also right when she said that the violets were the dead girl's soul. A love as great as that must have been fatal for a being so weak . . .

When night was already stretching out its mantle of shadow and the wind was bringing us the sound of the current, we arrived in Gross-Aspern, and from afar saw that little house hidden amidst the leaves, lonely and sad, since the doves no longer caressed it now but fled frightened when that pure soul passed flying alongside them . . .

Reverie

ONE afternoon in the month of May, an afternoon of the kind that smiles, and flaunts a blue, serene, clear sky as the sun's last rays launch their trembling reflection toward earth, I found myself sad without knowing why, contemplating such a beautiful scene.

My solitary garden, covered in perfumed flowers, with dashing palms and languid willows and cypresses; populated by groups of velvety butterflies, which in a mad whirlwind flew about the roses; visited from time to time by the birds, which, swinging on the branches of trees swayed by the breeze, gave their singing to the wind—sad sometimes like a lament, joyful at others, like the pearly laugh of an angel, flying through space—seemed to call me to its enclosure to meditate with the perfumed rose garden, or confuse my tears with the pearls tossed by the fountain, as it murmured tender songs in the middle of the garden.

❋

I entered into it and went to sit at the foot of a willow, which was surrounded by masses of violets and poppies.

I cut some of them, the symbol of modesty, whose perfume at once gentle and sweet penetrated my heart and filled it with a melancholy pleasure when I put them on my chest.

Sitting there, breathing, in solitude, I began to meditate on the peace and sweet tranquility of the tombs at eternal rest, listening all alone to the mournful sound of the icy wind in the branches of the cypress and willow, its only friends.

Thinking of this, I started to fall asleep. But a while later, I dreamed that an angel beat his wings and flew near me, and that his breath, when it brushed my face, froze it, along with my heart. Then he rested his hands on my brow and covered me with his wings . . .

He placed a kiss on my lips; and his breath—essence of violet—bathed my face.

That perfumed kiss, sweet, sublime, made me let out a sigh and, as if my spirit came detached from my body, it rushed toward the regions of the infinite.

And flying and flying with my white wings, which lashed the wind, I glimpsed the earth, that earth where I dreamed so much, looking like a black dot, an atom half-hidden in vague shadow, in the midst of the infinite grandeur that I contemplated.

I seemed, on coming near to the heavens, to hear sweet songs, which the angels sang in chorus, around God.

Night arrived at last, and as I approached the throne of His Majesty, I saw that some of those beings whose songs I had heard, inhabitants of the high regions, bore on their brows a bright star which, giving out a gentle light, bathed the earth where so many times I had contemplated a luminous trembling in a lake's peaceful waters, or on the silvery waves of the sea.

When they saw me enter, thousands of spirits gathered to carry me, as on a celestial wave, to the feet of the Supreme One, who placed his mighty right hand on my brow, making a bright star appear there. Me too! . . .

Intoxicated with my happiness, I seemed to hear the voices of the earth like a light murmur, as they perceived my appearance in the deep blue.

Lovers said: 'It is the bright star that protects our love.' Those who suffered: 'Its light brings us hope.' The happy: 'Our joy.' The poets: 'Our inspiration!'

A spirit then approached me—that of a being whom I loved and revered a great deal on earth—and said to me with affectionate yearning:

'You have wanted to grow wings, you have wanted your brow to give off light, you have asked it of me, and God, listening to my prayers, has given it to you. Now you have everything; you have arrived to where your desire can take you. Are you happy, my daughter?'

I could not answer, I flapped my wings, the star on my brow trembled, I let out a sigh of pleasure . . . and I awoke.

※

My dream had ended, and I found myself beneath the weight of reality. Night had already unfurled its mantle; the breeze froze my temples and on its wings brought to me a rhythmical sound from water falling in a wide bowl, as well as the perfumes of flowers, amidst which was prominent that of violets. The stars shone in the firmament, and their tranquil light made that place seem mournful, though in my dream I had believed it to be the sweet serene dwelling of my heart's joy and peace.

I stood up and, taking from my chest the violets I had placed there when I sat down—the only memory of my dreamed-of happiness—I put them away in a shrine, where I still preserve them.

The Water Nymphs

THERE were three of them. The oldest was named Coralina, the second Espumina and the youngest Perlina.

They lived in the depths of the sea, and as they were still too young, they had not left their cavern.

This area was immense, and although on the outside nothing could be seen but a rock covered with small shellfish, stones and algae, inside was a true palace.

The upper part served as a roof for the pretty dwelling of the water nymphs, and was covered with pearls, corals, shells and crystals. The ground was covered by the finest sand, in which little pieces of coral, precious stones and tiny golden rocks could be seen shining like stars in the sky.

Coralina was called by this name because she spent her days seated, as on a throne, atop a branch of coral.

Espumina, because she lived in a shell that the queen of the water nymphs created for her, so she could rest, touching the foam with her wand.

And Perlina, because she was accustomed to closing herself away with pearls inside the shell of an oyster, within its lovely nacre. What's more, she bore on her head a diadem of white pearls. From this came her name.

One day, when the three were seated together, Coralina said to her sisters:

'I am the oldest, I will see the world first and when I know it well, I will tell you whether or not you should also know it. Soon, very soon.'

'Why not now?'

'Because I am very young and lacking courage. So much is spoken about the world!'

'Oh, if I were in your place, Coralina, I would go now! I have such a great desire!'

'Would you do so in my place?'

'Of course! I am not afraid.'

'Do you really mean that?'

'Yes, and if you do not go soon, I will go.'

'No, Espumina, I will go, I promise you.'

'When?'

'Tomorrow.'

'Bravo!' said Espumina, clapping her hands.

The next day, when the sun was about to appear on the horizon, and red strokes could already be glimpsed on the beds of pearly clouds that waited like an empty throne to receive the first light, Espumina and Perlina embraced Coralina, who in regal dress prepared to leave her cavern for the first time to greet the world, that world she had still not seen except in dreams of water nymphs.

She then left the cavern and, when the sun was casting its first rays, sat on a rock, from there contemplating the city with its beautiful palaces, its magnificent towers, its splendid gardens and dazzling streetcars.

When she had contemplated it at her leisure, she moved a long way from the spot, but not so much that she did not see the city from afar as it began to wake.

The day passed in this way, watching all the movement of that human swell, hidden behind a rock just next to the beach.

In the afternoon, when the sun was already disappearing on the horizon and the first shadows of twilight were lowering to earth, enveloping it, a man came along the beach, the first she had seen up close, with his head down and walking very slowly.

He stopped almost in front of her and sat on a crag, holding his head in his hands.

After a while he stood up and, taking the zither he carried with him, began to sing to accompany it, a song that was extremely sad but also very sweet.

The water nymph, seeing a man for the first time and for the first time hearing a song, left the cavern, once he had finished, and presented herself without warning, asking:

'Why do you sing with such sadness?'

'Because I suffer,' he said.

'What are your sorrows?'

'I have loved a woman and she, the traitor, has deceived me.'

'Is this how women are?'

'Yes.'

'Then love me, as I am not one, yet am just as pretty or prettier than they are.'

'Who are you?'

'I am a water nymph.'

'What is your name?'

'My name is Coralina.'

'Coralina? Oh, but no corals can be as red as your lips.'

'Do you think I am beautiful?'

'Like an angel.'

'And do you love me?'

'Love you? Not yet, but I look at you with immense pleasure; you are so pretty!'

She turned her back on him and entered the cavern, leaving him startled and astonished.

The next day, in the afternoon, he returned to the same place and sang again while plucking the zither, but the water nymph did not emerge.

He came this way day after day, and still the water nymph did not appear.

Then he sang, calling to her and swearing to love her forever.

On the third day that he called her in this way, Coralina appeared and, approaching him, asked:

'Do you love me now?'

'With all my soul. And you?'

'I have always loved you.'

'Since when?'

'Since I first saw you.'

'And why didn't you come?'

'Because you didn't tell me you loved me.'

'And now that you know, will you always come?'

'Yes, always.'

Every afternoon he sang and, in love, she came to listen. One day, he said to her:

'Look, Coralina, I want to admire you out of the sea, like a woman. Come out and together we will travel the world and love each other forever, and you will be my wife. Do you want this?'

'Yes, I want it because you want it, but I will be unable to leave without permission from my queen. I will go look for her and ask her to make me a woman, and then I will return and we will go far away, wherever you like.'

He agreed and she disappeared into the abyss, leaving only some white foam remaining, which also soon disappeared.

Four days later, when he was singing again on the beach, the waters opened and Coralina emerged like a vision, setting out for the shore where very quickly she arrived, and going to sit by the singer's side.

'Are you a woman?' he asked her, astonished.

'Yes I am,' she answered.

'And how?'

'You must know that the queen of the water nymphs, who is godmother to my sisters and myself, promised us each one wish, whatever it may be. I went to look for her at her palace, and before her throne of a single pearl, I threw myself at her feet and asked her to make me a woman.

'She consented, and then called to Selín, one of the enormous and crafty fish under her command, ordering him to guide me, for as a woman I could now be eaten up by monsters. Sitting on Selín I arrived, and now here I am, a woman, never again a water nymph. Are you satisfied?'

'Yes, let us go. Very soon I will make you my wife, and proudly take you around the world, which will contemplate you with amazement.'

※

In vain did Espumina wait for the return of Coralina. She never came back.

'You must not doubt,' she said then to Perlina, 'that our sister must be so happy, so blessed, she has forgotten us. We must go too and see what she does not dare to leave, not even to come see us. I am ready to launch myself out from here, to see that sky reflected as blue here in the sea, those stars which look like eyes of fire through the waters, that world, in short, that sometimes I imagine as a paradise where one treads only flowers and gold dust, and at other times I imagine as a heap of debris and pebbles that destroy the feet, amongst which are the shreds of rich clothing.

'Would you like to come with me?'

'No, sister, I am not going. You go; and if that world is the paradise that you say, do not be like Coralina who forgot us. Detach yourself for a moment from the happiness you enjoy, and come take me there.'

'I promise you, little sister. What's more, you are very young and it's still better for you to wait. You are right not to follow me.'

The next day, Espumina kissed the forehead of Perlina, gave her a tight hug and, opening the door of the cavern, threw herself into the sea. By a rare coincidence, she came to land at the rock where Coralina had remained hidden away before meeting the singer.

Sitting there, she waited all day long for night to come and cloak her. Then she could come almost onto the beach, to see the city up close illuminated by golden mists, and hear people speak without them knowing she was there.

She lay down on the fine colorless sand on the rock and fell asleep, waiting for the disappearance of the sun and arrival of the shadows.

All at once, still asleep, she seemed to hear in the distance a sad song, very sad, which seemed more a lament than a song; but the notes that the instrument produced, still unknown to her, were so sweet and heartfelt that she shuddered and woke.

This was not a dream, it was the voice of a man and the harmonic notes of a zither, plucked by a master hand.

She came out of the cavern and, as if drawn by a magnetic force, went in search of the singer, who was on the beach nearby, seated on a crag that the waters endlessly kissed.

Without him seeing her, she came to him and, touching his shoulder, said, smiling:

'Why do you mourn this way?'

'Because a water nymph has deceived me, one who for my love, or so she told me, turned into a woman.'

'Come, tell me the whole story.'

'It is very simple. A woman whom I loved forgot me for another. Then I, sad, very sad, took my zither and here, far from the city which would perhaps mock my pain, came to tell my sorrows to the sea.

'A water nymph hidden between those rocks listened to me and, attracted by the music, came out, saw me and told me she loved me. I fell madly and blindly in love with her, begging her to come out so that together, she as my wife, I as her husband, would travel around the world. She agreed and, entering the depths of the sea, went to ask her queen to make her a woman.

'Three days later, I saw her appear. She emerged from the water, took me by the hand and said:

'"Now we can go. I am a woman, never again a water nymph."

'I, out of my mind with pleasure, brought her and lodged her in a palace, where I gave her flowers, gold and gemstones, along with slaves that sang or played instruments to send her to sleep.

'Very soon I was going to call her my wife, but, leaning out on the balcony one day, she saw a man pass, dressed with more luxury than a prince and riding a splendid horse. She fell in love with him, and he, who thought she was prettier than a dream, loved her too.

'One day I went to look for her and found only the slaves, who were crying, distressed by the disappearance of their lady.

'She had taken flight and abandoned me, the one for whom she had become a woman!

'Now that she had become one, she was like all of them: changeable and untrustworthy. Since then I have resolved never to love again, but sad, very sad, I come every night to sing here.'

'What was the water nymph called?'

'Her name was Coralina.'

'My sister!'

'Ah, she was your sister?'

'Yes.'

'It must be true, for you are as divinely beautiful as Coralina.'

'And you, what is your name?'

'My name is Armando.'

'What a lovely name.'

'Do you think so?'

'Yes, as lovely as you.'

'Ah, if that were so, your sister would not have forgotten me.'

'She forgot you because she was a woman . . . I would never forget you.'

'Do water nymphs not forget?'

'No, they can only love a single time.'

'Would you love me?'

'I love you.'

'What is your name?'

'Espumina.'

'The foam is less white than you are. You are truly very beautiful.'

'As much as what?'

'A lucky dream.'

'Would you love me?'

'No, because once you were a woman, you would stop loving me as your sister did.'

'Oh! then I will not be a woman. Come with me and I will love you for all eternity.'

'As a human I cannot enter that abyss.'

'I will ask my queen to grant me your entrance to the depths of the sea, where we have our palace.'

'Do you want this?'

'Yes.'

'And do you love me?'

'Yes.'

She sank into the waters, and Armando, with his gaze fixed on the point where he saw her disappear, asked himself if it had all been a dream, or if it was true that he had seen this water nymph from the sea.

After three days, just like her sister, Espumina appeared.

'And now?' Armando said, when he saw her.

'Are you going to follow me to my palace?'

'I will drown in the sea.'

'No, the queen has given me this pearl,' she said, showing it.

'What is it for?'

'You are going to drink it dissolved in water.'

She cupped a little water in her hand and dropped the pearl in, which immediately melted.

Then she brought the drink to the lips of the singer and said to him:

'Drink!'

He obeyed and took the concoction from the pretty hand of Espumina, who then said:

'Let's go. Now you can enter the sea, just like us.'

She took him by the hand and, pulling her to him, they jumped together into that great immensity.

Perlina, who had seen her arrive with that man she loved, embraced her on a day not long after, wiping away her tears.

'But why are you crying, my good Espumina? What is it? Aren't you happy?' she asked her.

'I am very miserable.'

'But what is missing?'

'Armando's love.'

'Did he die?'

'No, but he has stopped loving me and has left me for a siren.'

'How did that happen?'

'Ay, Perlina, this man who cried because two women had forgotten him found solace in my love, and I brought him here. He did not sing, he did not play his instrument, he lived contemplating me as I did him. But one day he took the zither he brought with him, and accompanying himself on it began to sing in his sweet voice, which trembled with love.

'The water nymphs and sirens came to listen, and I, full of pride, looked at all of them as they all jealously looked at me.

'Day after day he played and sang, and one day a siren arrived. He fell in love with her, and forgot me.

'Now I hear his beautiful voice and the notes of his zither in the distance, in the cavern of the sirens.

'Ah, my sister, how imperfect humans are! Instead of a heart they have a weather vane that constantly turns. Men complain of women, and women complain of men. All are the same!'

And the poor water nymph cried bitterly at her misfortune and was sad, and did not speak, or sing, or laugh.

Always mute, she lived within her shell.

One day Perlina went to visit the queen and, when she returned, she saw within the shell the body of her sister, who had just died and had begun to dissolve into a fine white foam.

A short time later, a pretty shell formed out of that foam.

Poor Perlina, now alone, wept a great deal and for a long time, due to these tragedies that the world had inflicted on her sisters.

One day she heard shouts, a great noise, many laughs; opening the door she asked what was happening, and a pretty water nymph, still a girl, answered:

'It's Armando, the man who sings and plays the zither and who loved your sister. He has forgotten his siren and fallen in love with another; but that one, who is very clever, complained to the queen, who, irritated by the disturbance and misfortunes the singer was responsible for, sent him to be returned once again to earth. Everyone ran after him and helped to throw him out, after punishing him harshly, which has given us much pleasure.'

Just as Armando was coming onto land, he saw a woman throw herself into the sea. She tumbled into the midst of the water nymphs, who shouted almost at once:

'Coralina!'

On hearing the name of her sister, Perlina grew frightened. She saw that the woman, most certainly dead, was none other than Coralina.

After falling in love with the one who had passed before the balcony of her house, she fled to accompany him and was married. But he, who quickly grew bored, left one day and did not return.

She, desperate, came then to the edge of the sea, climbed a rock, and at the same time that Armando was emerging, threw herself into the sea to die.

Perlina collected that dear body and coming before her sovereign, asked her in tears to take pity on her poor sister.

The queen consented; touching her wand to the poor dead water nymph, she made her into a black pearl.

Then she looked at Perlina and said:

'My good girl, there you have your sister turned into a black pearl, in memory of all she has suffered and the black clouds that have stained the sky of her happiness. Pearls like this are very few, very scarce; and to punish men, the cause of so many misfortunes, I will make them feel an ardent desire to possess them and a great work necessary to acquire them. Are you content?'

'Yes, my lady, and I am grateful to you.'

'And will you not ask me for the wish I have promised you?'

She meditated and then replied:

'Tomorrow I will come to ask it of you.'

Afterward she moved away, carrying the dear black pearl to the white shell where she was hiding.

With her head between her pretty hands, she spoke out loud to herself:

'My two sisters have died,' she said, 'and the world is the cause of their death. Must I expose myself in the same way, to suffer and perish like them? Is love, that good which all beings long for, truly happiness?

'There are very few happy people in the world, because different passions agitate in the human heart, some trivial, others great, very great, which destroy the primitive purity of love, some by reducing it to vile interest, others to vanity, others still to a simple distraction.

'Is there anyone who feels true love, enduring, great and immense? . . . Yes, love does exist this way, in beings whose souls come to be joined, and who thus launch themselves together toward the region of the ideal, where they dwell. Only in this way is it abiding and firm, even coming to have something of the divine.

'But, ay, it brings so much bitterness with it, if we chance to deceive ourselves.'

The next day Perlina went before the queen and said to her, kneeling at her feet:

'Queen and lady, I come in my turn to request the wish that you have promised me.'

'Speak. What do you want?' she asked.

'I want, my lady, to become a fairy. The fairy of the pearls.'

'And what will you do with this?'

'Oh, I have not yet finished! I want to be the fairy of the pearls, that is, their guardian. But I also want, my lady, for all those tears that pure and true love makes spill to be turned into white pearls, which I will keep in my possession.'

'Very well, my daughter, from this moment you shall have all that you desire,' the queen answered, placing her diadem on the head of the pretty water nymph, and in her hand the wand, a symbol of her dignity.

Since then the gentle fairy Perlina has gathered the tears of lovers and saved them, making crowns out of them for the weak who succumb to real passion.

Winter Song

RAIN FALLS. Black clouds cover the blue sky and hide the sun, the light that as it illuminates and heats bodies, heats and illuminates souls.

It is cold; there is darkness. There is also cold in the heart and snow in the soul.

Winter, harsh, with its snows and lashing cold north wind, withers the flowers.

In winter, days are dark as nights. In the sepulcher reigns eternal night.

When there is sweet sadness, one sleeps and then one dreams, and the dreams are rosy.

In the tomb, where one also sleeps, oh God, what will they be like, the dreams? When we wake, we smile at the memory of the delights seen in repose. Then we frown and our brows darken: we are joined to reality; the dreams were dreams, nothing more!

Within the tomb, is there no waking? Do not wounding realities come after fabricated illusions? There will be no perfumes of flowers, gleams of stars, light at dawn, angelic laughter, celestial heat in the spirit. Oh! souls surely do not have wintry fogs, withered flowers, clouds that hide bright stars, squalls that tear apart little boats, thorns or darts for the heart, or brambles that tear off the feathers of innocent doves.

In this world, after the warmth of the sun during the day and the silvery radiance of the moon, luminous rays of stars and gentle murmurs during the nights of spring and summer, winter arrives. The winter that brings cold and withers flowers and illusions, and with them life!

Winter is sad, it is somber for those who do not have heat to comfort the body and joyful illusions to enliven the soul.

But blessed are you, old Winter, when one hears the rain slowly falling, and the dense fog surrounds us and the cold arrives with that idle ache that overcomes us, while wrapped in soft furs, we feel the light in our soul that is lacking in nature, and the spring that is moving away, in our hearts.

We hear the birds sing, the bees buzz, the white lilies sway waggishly on their stalks, we breathe in the perfume of the heliotropes and jasmines, we hear the murmur of the breeze in the tall trees and see the pearly dew that moistens the green lawn. All that, within our heart.

Is there snow? Welcome! How one sees that rain of swan feathers turn the landscape white!

Is it cold? One doesn't feel it: within the chest is a bonfire that gives life, heat, light.

Is everything gloomy, the roses withered, the trees without leaves?

The soul is smiling. There, flowers exist whose perfume intoxicates, there divine plants are born, grow and are beautiful; there, music, harmony, and verse enliven, while with our eyes half-closed, we dream and are able to see, behind the gray mantle of the sky, the pink and blue of dawn, with its twilight smile.

It is cold and it rains and snows. At the theater, at the ball, where thousands upon thousands of lights shine. In the hearths the fire burns; the music vibrates in triumph, and in the midst of playful laughter, one dances the waltzes there that give vertigo, while illusions fly and twirl about like mad butterflies. Some eyes shine black and deep, others blue and tender; and rosy lips quiver, murmuring sweet words.

And one hears the rain fall, and under the streetlights one sees the snow like a silver sheet, and one says meanwhile, 'How lovely!'

How lovely! Yes, seen thus Winter is very beautiful. But how horrible when it is felt in the heart and reigns in the soul, and brings us the cold that kills. It passes and Spring returns, and still, it does not go away.

But when the roses do not wither and the butterflies do not stop flying, in the garden of daydream, it is splendid to see the roofs turn white, and the trees without leaves and the leaden sky. Joyful, the rhythmic sound of the rain caresses the ear.

Blessed are you, old Winter!

The Gold and the Copper

THE gold inhabited the main building: the copper the porter's lodge.

It was truly a beautiful palace, very beautiful. Anything that refinement, art and style could invent was there in the most diverse forms.

The marquises Roberto and Cristine resided there. Oh! they were rich, very rich. Dressed always in silk and splendor, covered in jewels and precious stones during the day and lying at night between cushions of feathers, soft white furs and silk coverlets, they lived well.

They went to the theater, were constantly served sumptuous meals, went on pleasure trips in a carriage through the forest and Elysian Fields, attended the races and great balls, received constant greetings from the very poorest, listened as to the buzz of the mob of flatterers who always spoke sickly-sweet words, and they grew bored.

Their son Carlos Federico, the little future marquis, was still not a year old and was already amusing and so cute! He was a delicate flower in bud.

His skin was rosy and smooth, his red lips were always smiling; his lovely blue eyes were big and lively and his little head was shaped by infinite tiny curls, the color of the gold he would inherit.

To say that they loved him would be to put it lightly; his parents worshipped him.

How the little one lived, covered in very rich ornaments and splendid jewels! His nappies were of smooth silk, and he wore either little caps or very white furs or precious lace, according to the season.

If the boy cried, one sang and played to make him laugh, or gave him toys of great value that he broke right away, to obtain others.

Below, in the porter's lodge of the same palace, the porter Manuel and his wife Rosa, who were extremely poor, worked all day long. Manuel went up and down, sometimes to bring a message, at other times the mail.

Rosa sewed and stitched, patching their very poor-quality clothing made of linen and washing it until it was whiter than snow. She seasoned her few and coarse foodstuffs in such a way that they came to seem tasty and even succulent, and she cleaned and swept their room, singing without cease all day long. They loved each other very much. Manuel and Rosa were very poor, and only coins of copper touched their hands, but they were happy.

Their son, little Luis, was a little less than a year old, like the son of the marquises.

He was not white like the other, but to his dark color the burning red of his cheeks and lips added much beauty. His black eyes were almond-shaped, and his head of almost black, chestnut-colored hair was curly and soft.

He always laughed; he never cried. He wore a little cotton shirt, which was very white, yes indeed, nappies of linen, and, instead of a cap, a handkerchief knotted round his head.

Was his mother busy? She put him on the ground on a little mattress of straw that she herself had made, and there, very quietly, he played and shimmied and laughed holding a piece of a doll without a head that Manuel had picked up from the trash, the remains of one that the little marquis had broken.

When Rosa had finished, she took him in her arms and played with him and caressed him, kissed him, made him dance on her knees and spoke to him any sugary-sweet phrase she found at hand to interpret her love.

At night he slept in the arms of his father, who then took him to his little straw mattress, even covering him with his own clothes so that he was not cold in winter.

When some copper coin could be freed by virtue of scrimping, Rosa went running and brought ribbons and ordinary fabrics to make him a little cap for Sundays, and then, crazy with joy and full of vanity, she carried him outside so that the whole world could admire him in his fancy dress, and she sang without cease, and he smiled, and she kissed her little brown boy.

The poor boy got sick one day, and his mother, in tears because she did not have the means to call a doctor, went to look for something to make an infusion, but the fever did not go down, and they cried. They gave him other medicines, the kind that cost very little, and the boy recovered his health and returned to being glowing and robust; his parents went back to being happy.

The little marquis bacame sick, in his turn; just like Luis, he had fever. They called the doctor, the servants went running, medicines abounded. The boy grew worse. A call was made to the doctors, they argued a lot, they prescribed and prescribed and gave the poor boy thousands upon thousands of drugs, but on the third day he died.

His parents cried, moaned and despaired. The cold little body of poor Carlos Federico was dazzling in velvets, gold and, above all, very valuable jewels.

Rosa, holding her little Luis in her arms, with her head wrapped in a black handkerchief as a sign of mourning and her white cotton clothing, went to contemplate the little marquis. After she had looked at him for a long time and admired him still longer, she took her husband by the hand and exclaimed:

'How much poverty, adorned by opulence!'

'You are right,' he answered. 'And our treasure is not known or seen because he goes about covered by poverty.'

He took Rosa and their son Luis in his arms, and they went away, giving each other many kisses.

❋

The next day was the burial. Oh! it was splendid. What pomp was displayed, what gold flowed, to bring the little marquis with dignity to the black and somber shaft where he, just like his luxurious clothing, would turn to dust.

While the poor parents were returning from the cemetery, Manuel, still embracing his little one, went to the funeral to hand over the many cards that had arrived to express the grief of their friends and flatterers.

For the first time since those porters had lived there, the charming boy, poorly dressed but healthy and laughing, was noticed.

The marquis looked at him full of envy, and asked the father:

'Whose boy is this?'

'He is ours, señor marquis.'

'Do you love him a great deal?'

'We adore him, señor.'

'And are you happy?'

'Very much so. We do not want for anything.'

'Then are you rich?'

'No, señor, our treasure and our joy is the love that Rosa and I have, and that we have for our Luis. We work hard, we live very poorly, but we are always content. We are happy.'

'Ay! You are right. We amidst the gold and abundance only grow bored. We adored our son and he has died.

Joy has fled forever from our side. What are we today? Poor, poorer than you. It is not where gold is that there is happiness and joy! Take this,' he then added, giving to Manuel four gold coins. 'Take this gold that for us no longer shines and has not prevented us from being so miserable, and use it to give your son more security and comfort. Enjoy and you will be even happier.'

Gold, for the first time in the life of that married couple, penetrated into that room where copper dwelled, but also peace and happiness.

That winter Luis slept wrapped in soft furs like a noble, and in summer he had a little cap with ribbons and a complete little outfit. And he smiled, and his parents, crazed with happiness, took him for a stroll and kissed him and sang, making him jump between their arms.

Humanzor

D. is a pretty little town where the traveler is not very comfortable, but where the inhabitants are always pleased and so agreeable that they make one forget the backward conditions in which they live.

It is located in a valley and surrounded by mountains and hills, eternally green. Very close by is the forest where the hollies and oaks rustle their majestic heads and the pines, firs and poplars grow in abundance, in messy ensemble.

When the sun appears on the horizon, sending its golden reflection over the plains and hillocks, the shepherds can be seen with their dogs alongside, some watching over the sheep, others the cows; singing, playing reed flutes or shouting as they brand the herd.

Their little houses, the majority made of straw, are separated by very beautiful orchards, where the banana tree with its yellowish bunches, the orange tree with its white blossoms, and the coconut tree with its crown of palm and big fruit give a fresh and fragrant shade.

Three tiled houses are treated as sumptuous palaces. The first is that of the priest; the second that of the

Mayor and the last, the best, that of a particular rich man, owner of an estate as well as the town hotel.

This last house, which has several halls and ample corridors, and is decorated with bizarre paintings by some extravagant painter, is the delight of all, for there dances are given, and, furthermore, during Easter it is rented to acrobats and puppeteers for their performances.

The hotel, which looks like a room from that house, is composed of a medium-sized hall where coffee, wine and light refreshments are served, and a long, narrow dining room, where one sees an unsteady table pushed against the wall and six chairs that surround it on three sides; in addition, there are two old and dirty benches. Three small rooms, whitened with lime, serve to lodge travelers, who find a cot there with leather straps instead of a mattress, a hammock full of holes, a chair made of sticks, and a table that does double duty as a dresser and washstand.

Roasted potatoes, bananas, cheese, cooked legumes and a piece of mutton make up the menu at that inn for guests. Then come the rich steaming coffee and the plate of fruit, and lunch is over.

At night there is music, composed of a guitar, two flutes, a drum, two horns and a kind of tambourine that the daughter of the hotel manager plays.

And they are all happy there, and he who arrives and forgets the inconveniences feels happy too.

We arrived in D. and asked a man where we could find lodging that would accommodate us.

He offered to serve us as a guide to bring us to the hotel, and so he did, remaining settled by his own means in a tiny room that the owner of the establishment kept for this end.

In the morning, following the day of our arrival, we visited the whole town and in the afternoon we climbed the hill, from which one could glimpse the sea from one side, and from the other the city with its big houses, palaces and parks.

It was a magnificent view, and we were there until the setting of the sun, which went to hide itself as if it were sinking into the waters of the sea, which in the reflections of the last rays at times seemed a sheet of silver, at others a lake of blood.

We then began to descend and, when we entered the town, there could now be heard from afar the sad measures of shepherds' flutes and the songs of young girls.

Eight days must have passed since we'd arrived, for which reason we were already known and knew the majority of the inhabitants, who gathered together with us every afternoon after the meal, to speak with us and ask us to describe for them the amusements of the city, its houses and, above all, its theatrical performances.

One of those afternoons we went for a stroll with several villagers, among which were the daughter of the hotel manager whom they called *señorita* for being the richest in the place, and the old master of the school, who was called Jaime and was an excellent man.

We did a few turns and went afterward to sit in a small, pretty square, where an old holm oak with fresh ivy stuck to its trunk gave a generous shadow.

I then saw, for the first time since our arrival, a house that was rather large and not ugly, but somewhat run-down, locked up and set apart from the rest, all of which attracted my attention. Pointing to it, I asked:

'And that silent and hidden house, to whom does it belong?'

All turned their heads in the direction I pointed, and the old master answered me:

'That house belongs to no one, and since the blood of Humanzor spilled over its stones, no one has returned to it. That man inspired terror alongside affection; one fears even his shadow, and for this reason no one goes there.'

'Who is this Humanzor? Tell me his story,' I said.

'I will tell you, if you like, but let us go to the center of the plaza, for here it is already very dark, if that is alright with you.'

We went to take shelter under the pale and tender cloak of the moon.

'Go on, Jaime my friend,' I said to him, 'I am impatient to hear you.'

'It will take a long time, my lady,' he answered.

'So much the better,' I replied.

'In that case, let us turn to the incident.

'I will begin by telling you that Humanzor was left an orphan at eight years of age, and that, although he had two uncles, the boy was thrown completely upon his own devices, for neither of the two wanted to take responsibility for him. An old man then took him into his service; but he treated him in a brutal way, and one night the poor defenseless orphan abandoned that

77

home and wandered for two days, looking in vain for someone to employ him.

'Exhausted at last by hunger and cold, he knocked at the doors of several houses and begged for their inhabitants' charity. But all denied him and slammed the door in his face.

'A short time afterward he rolled senseless through the damp grass and would no doubt have perished were it not for a merciful shepherd, an orphan like himself, but older, who picked him up and brought him to his humble straw mattress, where he managed to warm him, and shared with him his piece of black bread. It was something, and the poor boy lived.

'He remained alongside that companion who was good to him, always helping him with his tasks.

'But his young protector died three years later, and once again he was without help.

'He resolved to go from the town to the city, not knowing how unhappy great cities are for the wretched destitute.

'One day after having arrived there, mad, blind with weakness and hunger, he stole a few coins from a miserly old lady, with which he bought a piece of bread and cheese that he gobbled down with infinite longing. He had now taken his first false step.

'He was discovered and the police shut him away under lock and key. They interrogated him and he answered with a wild voice, very strange for his young age:

'"I have stolen so as not to die of hunger. I asked for work and did not find it, I asked for alms and did

78

not find them either; so I had to steal or die. I stole, I repeat, so as not to die."

'He was condemned to prison for two months, which was enough time for the boy to transform into a man. The dark and gloomy jail, the hard black bread and the old stale water they gave to him, a poor and unfortunate boy, whose only crime was not to have had the affectionate hand of a father to help guide him through the world, made him meditate on the unfairness of his luck. An infinite bitterness filled his heart, and from a loving and sensitive child, he turned hard and cruel.

'How many beings like this, perhaps born for good, become wicked by the injustice of fate! The poor boy, instructed on the path of good and having found protection, would have become a worthy man.

'When he left his prison, he disappeared for a long time, and it was not known until recently that during this period he was under the protection of a handful of highwaymen who adopted him, teaching him the profession with great profit on his part.

'Eight years after the death of his parents and four after his departure from the town, that is, when he was already sixteen years old, he came to make his appearance again.

'He was a truly beautiful young man, and was as developed as if he were twenty-five. His white skin had a matte paleness; his extremely dark hair fell in beautiful ringlets around his wide, clear forehead; his black eyes, also large, had a wild expression of ferocity and sometimes seemed to dilate their pupils, which shone like a lightning flash of concentrated hate; on his thin red lips a smile of bitter irony constantly idled, accentuated even more by the shadow given to his upper lip by the black down that had begun to cover it.

'He was quite tall and sturdy; his muscles were those of an athlete. He was imposing with his presence, and even more so with his fierce look.

'Now he was not the ragged boy of four years before. Just the opposite, he dressed with elegance and even too much luxury.

'Hardly had he arrived before they learned that this great lord was none other than Humanzor, and all hurried to greet him and offer him their services.

'When he no longer needed them! He received them with coldness and contempt and did not visit anyone. He only went to the cemetery and went down there on his knees, first before the tomb of his parents, then before that of that humble shepherd who had sheltered him when, nearly dead of hunger and cold, he had fallen senseless on the damp grass.

'Over both were shed tears of sincere love from those ever-dry and gloomy eyes.

'Eight days he remained there, and then one night he left, without anyone seeing him go.

'Six months had passed since his departure. Easter, which is the time of this town's amusements, approached.

'Following our customs, we prepared several acts, and left for the city with the aim of bringing musicians for an orchestra as well as acrobats, little traveling theater acts and other minor diversions.

80

'One of those days, walking through the city, we saw several groups everywhere, speaking with great liveliness. It piqued our curiosity, and we decided to approach one composed of women and listen. But they, no doubt believing us to be from there, asked us almost at once and with great cries:

'"What's the news?"

'"Have the police already begun to move?"

'"Are they going to take everything we possess?"

'And like these, another thousand questions, which we did not understand one bit. This I expressed to them, and then one of them, who seemed more alarmed and whom all had surrounded when we arrived, lifted her arms and said to me with an air of terror:

'"Do you truly not know what is happening?"

'"That is right, my lady,' I answered her, 'and I beg you to tell us, for we are frightened even though we do not know the cause."

'"God from heaven!" she said, "know that shortly, if the police do not begin to get moving, they are going to leave us in the street and reduce the city to ashes."

'"Who will?" one of ours timidly asked.

'"The bandits captained by Humanzor."

'"Humanzor!" we all repeated, looking at one another in astonishment.

'"Yes, Humanzor, that wild man who, according to what is said, comes from the town of D., and who has pounced like a hungry wolf on all places. Yesterday he stole ten thousand duros of gold from Señor Gonzalo de la Palma, the banker."

'"And when did that man reappear?" I asked.

'"Oh! for six months now he has been traveling through the country. He and his companions always rob the rich, that is true: the poor never, and it's even said that the boys protect him."

'"In that case, he does not flee, and pulls the beards of the police," I told her.

'"Yes, señor, it seems they have a pact with the devil. He goes freely everywhere, yet they cannot manage to get the cuffs on him.

'We continued on our way, amazed at all we had just heard, and in the end decided to enter a restaurant as planned, for lunch.

'There we found a group of gentlemen arranged with exquisite luxury.

'All were dressed in fine black cloth, boots of patent leather, white ties and kidskin gloves that on some were lilac and others gray. The majority held in their hand a little whip, with a handle of gold or shell.

'They listened with great attention to one man who had his back turned to the door. We saw only that his hand, white and slim, flaunted an enormous solitaire diamond that must have been of great value.'

The Glass Woman

AHMED WALLA KAND, prince of one of the largest sections of Hindustan still unconquered by the Europeans, rose to the throne of his elders when he was twenty-five years old.

A month after taking possession of the kingdom, he ordered that freedom be given to the women of the harem, and at the same time ordered that others, the loveliest of his kingdom and the markets of Asia, be purchased and brought to his presence. When his vassals had done so, they advised him and two days later his palace was overwhelmed by a mass of women, whose splendid beauty made them rivals.

Here were Persians, there Nubians, a little further along Circassians and Arabs, all richly decked out, some flaunting dazzling black eyes, others red lips tinted like the flower of the turpentine tree, still others heads of hair, the splendid mantle given to them by nature, more splendid than the mantle of royalty.

All, one by one, were brought before the prince, who sent them to the harem or ordered them to be given freedom according to the better or worse impression these female slaves' charms made on him.

After a year had passed, however, he no longer visited the harem, as he no longer wanted anything. He had grown bored.

His orgies, his museums, his hunts, all that he had enjoyed in excess now left him indifferent.

He called to his wise men, and under their guidance gave himself over completely to the study of European languages, science and his own religion, desiring in this way to pay due homage to the gods.

He made genuine progress in a short time, above all in religion.

When he believed that he knew enough on the subject, he made great improvements to the temples and gave great encouragements to worship. However, he soon grew bored with this too.

He then embarked on a long journey, which began in the European colonies of India. He moved on to Persia, Turkey and Arabia, where he stopped and returned immediately, tired of traveling. He shut himself away in his palace, prisoner to a great melancholy.

When he and his retinue returned, nothing was spoken of but a woman of glass which the enchanter Marust kept in his possession. According to what was said, the charm would be broken and she would return to being a woman, a very lovely woman, the day she came to love and be loved by a man.

This came to the ears of Ahmed, and immediately he sent for Marust, ordering him, once in his presence, to speak all that he knew about the matter.

'Prince and lord,' said Marust, bowing three times and crossing both hands over his chest; 'you must know that just over three months ago, while in the study where I carry out my work, I saw Thur the enchanter, who died twenty-five years ago, appear amidst a cloud of smoke, holding the hand of a woman covered with a veil.

'Directing himself to me, he said:

'"Marust, you were my disciple, and I wish for you to obey me today as you did before. Swear to me by the goddess to do what I order."

'"Master," I answered him, "I swear to you."

'"Good; if you break your word, Shiva will punish you," he said.

'He then directed himself to the covered one, who had been left slightly behind him, and pulled off her veil, to expose the most beautiful woman that one can see or dream about. He remained absorbed in contemplation.

'"Marust," he said again, "this beautiful woman that you see also possesses a heart of bronze; at her feet she has seen princes, kings and emperors die, and has never softened. Shiva has grown irritated and ordered me to punish her."

'He then reached out his arm, touched the chest of the woman with his magic wand and pronounced the mysterious words that instantly turned her into a statue of dark glass.

'"You will keep her," he said to me, "and let the whole world know that her punishment will come to an end the day that being loved, she loves in return.

The day that she looks with gentle eyes at a man, the glass will break into pieces and she will reappear, lovelier than ever. If she loves that man, she will be free of punishment; if she does not love him, she will go back under her layer of glass. Warn those who desire her to be very careful, for the slightest rupture they make to her will mean a death sentence for both. I recommend you to look after her well."

'Then he waved in a gesture of farewell and disappeared, leaving the beautiful statue by my side.

'When the impression of terror that all this had caused in me dissipated, I took that woman into my arms and placed her in a niche, afraid of the misfortune that Thur had warned me about if she came to break. Immediately afterward, I notified your subjects of all that has happened to me.

'Since that day all the lords in our kingdom have visited the poor enchanted one, a great number of them remaining captivated by the shroud of such marvelous beauty.

'This, lord and sovereign, is what I have to tell you, and now I await the orders that you will be so good as to give me.'

The enchanter bowed again three times and waited for permission to retire, which the prince gave.

With his head bowed, Ahmed stayed there for a few moments ordering one of his vassals to prepare his carriage, as he would go out.

When he was all ready, he climbed in. Surrounded by guards, he ordered Marust to guide him to his house, and he was led there. Leaving everything at the door, he went in with the enchanter, who brought him before the statue.

He contemplated her in silence for a long time, examining her lovely hands, her tiny feet, and a face that, though melancholy, possessed such strange beauty, all in a color so dark.

In passionate tones he then spoke to her, for although no sound came from her lips, he knew through Marust that in spite of being made of glass she heard, saw and felt perfectly.

She remained impassive, and he even thought that she looked disdainful.

He left at last, but remained worried, wondering why it was that if all sang of his beauty, and no woman had ever resisted him, this one looked at him with indifference, even contempt.

The next day he returned, and did so every day for a month, at the end of which he was hopelessly in love with the scornful woman.

Throwing himself before her, he kissed her feet and dress, wept and pleaded her for love.

She remained mute and impassive.

He then asked Marust to let him bring her to his palace, offering him treasure in exchange, as well as free entrance to see the enchanted one whenever he liked.

Marust agreed, and the woman of glass was placed between cushions of silk and gold and solemnly brought to the palace, with Ahmed traveling on foot alongside.

He had made preparations to receive her in the best room in the palace, adorning it with dazzling luxury. Twenty slaves, picked out by him from amongst the most lovely, remained by her side as guardians. At night he placed her with the greatest care in a bed whose drapery and coverings were changed every day, always ordering the best and newest things. During the day, he placed her in a kind of seat of honor circled by flowers and precious stones; at her feet, on a cushion, he ordered his own crown to be placed.

He did not leave the place, always watching her, crying and swearing to love her forever.

One day, while he was kneeling at her feet, Marust entered and he called him to his side.

'Marust, Marust,' he shouted, 'this woman is a rock, I am dying of love, I consume myself for her and she does not look at me, she despises me.'

He burst into tears, and in the midst of his weeping, said again to the charmer:

'Listen, Marust, listen my friend, if this woman loved me, for her I would leave my throne, my religion, if she did not share it, my language, my country. Oh! may she love me, may she love me and I will be her slave!'

'You say, lord, that for her you would leave your kingdom and your form of worship?'

'Yes, yes, all of it I would leave for her.'

'You would become a Protestant if she were?'

'I would, yes, a thousand times over!'

'A Catholic?'

'That too. I would do anything, anything; do not drive me to despair, Marust, I have told you already and I repeat: I will be her slave.'

'Lord, would you leave your women, all so lovely, for one alone, and give yourself exclusively to her?'

'Oh yes! What do all those who die for a look of mine matter to me, when this one is costing me my life and doesn't wish to hear me? If some day she comes to love me, all my life I would fear to lose her. Oh! how certain it is that we only value what is difficult to obtain, and what is impossible drives us mad. What can I do to prove my love to her, so that she yields to my pleas?'

'Do, lord, all that your heart dictates, and perhaps she will become human.'

Three more months passed, six months, a year, and for all his efforts, all that he cried, pleaded and threw himself at the feet of that woman, the glass did not break.

This provoked such desperation in the prince that one day he went to her, and swore in the presence of the charmer that beginning from that day, he would taste no more food of any kind, for he wanted to die slowly so as to contemplate her until the last moment, then call her ungrateful, before expiring.

He put his promise into practice, shutting himself away in his study next to hers, and remained seated there, sleeping neither day nor night. Every so often he opened the door joining the two rooms and, silent and sad, came to contemplate her and kiss her feet.

A day and a night had passed without him tasting anything, without him closing his eyes. The first rays of the sun pierced into the palace and came to illuminate the room, in the middle of which, among the softest and richest linens, lying down amongst the softest cushions, was the woman, or rather, the statue of glass.

Ahmed, sitting in his room on a gold and ornate seat of honor made of precious stones, wept to have her very beautiful head adorned with glossy black hair resting in the palm of his hand.

All of a sudden a horrible sound, like something shattering, wounded his ears and left him terrified.

He stood up, half-crazed, and ran to see what was happening, shaking with fear for his statue.

Entering and approaching the bed, he stopped in mute admiration and pleasure when, in the midst of the soft linens and cushions, lying down and smiling, he saw a woman of an entirely new beauty.

Hundreds of pieces of dark glass were scattered through the entire room, even on the bed.

Ahmed lowered his eyes before the fascinating gaze of that woman and, silent and trembling, came to lower himself on his knees before her feet.

Then she sat up and stretched out her soft white hand, on whose very slim fingers the nails were rose-colored and delicate:

'Get up, my friend,' she said to him.

He took this hand, covering it with kisses and tears, and collapsed on the ground.

When she saw him fall, she shouted for help. Her slaves, who had previously served to remove the statue from the bed, came running, but drew back frightened when they saw a woman so supremely beautiful instead of glass, and the prince in a faint or perhaps dead.

'Come, my friends,' she said to them, 'come and bring your lord to his bed and may the doctors arrive soon; in the meantime, dress me.'

They ran to obey her orders, and shortly she saw herself clad in silk, gold and precious stones by the side of the prince, who did not take long to come round. He called to the ungrateful one, who hurried to appear, smiling in the most seductive way.

When he saw her, he jumped from the bed and threw himself on his knees, kissing her mantle and her hand, crazed, blinded with love.

She begged him to take nourishment, for weakness given a shock had been the cause of his fainting.

He consented, sitting by her side and asking the slaves to serve him.

For eight days there were celebrations throughout all the kingdom, in honor of that woman.

However, she did not say to Ahmed that she loved him, which once again made him suffer, as he was blind with love for her, now even more than before the charm had been lifted.

One day he came to her and, taking her white and perfumed hand covered with dimples between his, said with sadness:

'Tell me, if you do not love me, why did you break your charm thus preventing me from dying? What do you want from me, in exchange for your love? Speak and tell me everything; if you will not love me, I will die.'

'No, Ahmed,' she answered, 'I do not want you to die, for I will love you very much if you are obliging to me.'

'Ask, ask anything in exchange for your love, and I will give it to you, up to the impossible.'

'Will you love a woman who does not share your beliefs?'

'If that woman is you, I will love her and believe in what she believes, for her version of devotion must be the true one, so lovely are the women who follow it.'

'Will you become a Catholic?'

'Are you a Catholic?'

'Yes.'

'Then I already am one too.'

'Would you leave your kingdom to follow me? Your vassals?'

'When you go, I will go, and instead of having vassals, I will be yours.'

'Thank you, Ahmed. I will compensate you, if my love is sufficient to compensate you. Will you leave your women and take me as your only one, eternally, according to the European laws?'

'Oh, yes! only you and you alone for me.'

'Very well, Ahmed, gather your gold and jewels and in silence call your brother. Hand over the command to him and let us go to the English colonies.'

Eight days later, Ahmed left with that woman and ten slaves, bringing his riches to Calcutta, where they settled down without their vassals knowing of their departure, until they were informed by the new prince, Ahmed's brother. Angry with Marust, they went looking for him to bring about his death, but he, who had foreseen this reaction, had also already left with his riches for some other place.

Ahmed spent two years in Calcutta, waiting for that woman to desire to join him in union.

During that period he learned French and English perfectly, took Catholicism for his religion and received the name William at the baptismal font.

At the end of this time, when she saw that the blindfold placed by ignorance over his eyes no longer existed, she had him call at her house and, sitting beside him, said:

'Guillermo, do you still love me?'

'What do you mean, still?' he answered. 'When have I stopped loving you, if every day I love you more and in proportion to your ingratitude toward me?'

'No, I am not ungrateful, just the opposite: I have been afraid to lose you, and for that reason have wanted to test you. I have also wanted to make you see everything as it truly is, which has occurred. I am English, the daughter of the Marquis de Wisp, as well as the widow of the Duke of Alta-Mira, of Spanish origin, with whom they united me at the age of fifteen years entirely against my will and without my ever loving him. After six months of marriage he died, and I was left free and extremely rich.

'I wanted to travel and came here after visiting nearly all of Europe.

'One day I saw you, just after you had assumed the throne, traveling to distract yourself, bored with all pleasure. I fell in love with you then, and promised myself to make you love me.

'From that moment, I began to study your language and went about disguised as an Arab in your kingdom, to which I saw you return with an even greater weariness.

'I then went to see Marust, promising him a purse full of gold if he did everything that I told him, and another if everything turned out well for me.

'He accepted, and I requested him to have the statue made in Europe, and to have it sent to me immediately afterward. I told him what he must say to you, and ordered him to tell me everything that you did and said, at all times, including even the slightest details. He fulfilled his word with great zeal and precision, and thus I learned of your resolution to let yourself die of hunger.

'Then I disguised myself in your clothing, and in this way penetrated to the location of the statue, where I slipped on its clothes, lay down on the cushions and struck a blow to the statue which, delicate as it was, exploded into a thousand pieces. The rest you already know.'

'Do you love me still?'

'I adore you.'

'Tomorrow I will be your wife and then we will go to England.'

Eight days later, now united, they embarked in the direction of the British Isles.

The duchess, who was very beloved by the king, presented her husband before the court and told her story.

The king, in whom the cleverness of that woman produced true admiration, and desiring to demonstrate to the prince his satisfaction at seeing him his subject, conceded to him the title of prince of British India.

Nevertheless, no one referred to the princess by her title, but by Mira the Oriental, from her old title Alta-Mira.

Delirum, or Sonata

GO on, go on, white daydreams! Images of joy that have borne away time, golden illusions, smiling hopes, perfumed memories! Oh, go on, go on, kiss my forehead! and then, then, goodbye until tomorrow, when you will appear again.

Like that . . . oh what delight!

The music that quivers in my ears has those notes of a harp, and is gentle and brings a memory wrapped in its harmony! Yes, it is the same: On its mysterious wave roll its confused echoes, the sweet notes of that loving voice.

The lights that give off yellowish reflections like the thousand bright stars and the laughter of charming couples; the intoxicating perfume of the flowers that voluptuously tremble in the blue vases of Bohemia crystal and the bows of white silk that move with the wind . . . Oh! yes, there I see his figure that stands out trembling and passionate amidst that setting from the past.

And his eyes are gentle! and they look profoundly, they look to the depth of my unconscious soul. And his lips smile, oh! and I hear his words of fire that scorch my heart.

Go on, go on, let me see you, images of love.

Go on yet one more time, even if afterward you go back to sink into the shadows!

Refresh with that life-giving breath of memory and vision my feverish head; soothe my heart that howls with pain and sorrow.

Ah! may I see you shine as I see that bright star that stands out pale amidst the scattered clouds of the afternoon, a mix of colors: caress of the sun on the white clouds; kisses of the night in space!

Go on through the black veil that sadness wraps round my soul, as the smiling moon passes, illuminating and leaving its gleaming trail like atoms of itself, through the mournful immensity.

And then, why not? as after the flight of the moon comes the rosy dawn and after the dawn the sun, the red lord that embodies the day; thus after the languor of a pale and gentle memory, one of those that sends the angels to sleep, come, come, come and burn my heart, burn my mind and even my lips if they smile, O you rays from a sun in ardent summer which fleetingly gleamed, and which time and distance have faded.

Send my soul to sleep like those genies of the night who throw to earth handfuls of poppies, to make humanity drowsy!

Let me sleep, may I sleep forever until the time that has borne away my hopes comes to wake me at the doors of my happiness, that once again it has found and I have lost at the edge of the tomb.

Ah, do not go yet: continue, continue parading by, caressing and smiling memories; take the form that you will incarnate one day.

Fly around me, speak to me thus in that voice of angelic music, perfume my existence like flowers in the wind; give my soul color like the sunbeam to the weak plant!

Like that, like that . . .

CPSIA information can be obtained
at www.ICGtesting.com
Printed in the USA
LVHW051505050819
626562LV00005B/803

9 781645 250067